For Bea —J.A.
For Sue —A.M.

Text copyright © 2020 by Jennifer Adams
Illustrations copyright © 2020 by Alea Marley
Published by Roaring Brook Press
Roaring Brook Press is a division of Holtzbrinck Publishing Holdings Limited Partnership
120 Broadway, New York, NY 10271
mackids.com

Library of Congress Control Number: 2019948824

ISBN: 978-1-250-31004-0

Our books may be purchased in bulk for promotional, educational, or business use. Please contact your local
bookseller or the Macmillan Corporate and Premium Sales Department at (800) 221-7945 ext. 5442 or by
email at MacmillanSpecialMarkets@macmillan.com.

First edition, 2020
Book design by Monique Sterling
Printed in China by Hung Hing Off-set Printing Co. Ltd.,
Heshan City, Guangdong Province

1 3 5 7 9 10 8 6 4 2

Goodnight,
LITTLE DANCER

BY Jennifer Adams

ILLUSTRATED BY

Alea Marley

Roaring Brook Press
New York

time for bed now, *little dancer*.

Time to tell the world *goodnight*.

Let down your bun, shake out your hair.

Breathe in, relax, and dim the light.

Goodnight, ribbons.

Goodnight, slippers.

Goodnight, floors and mirror and barre.

You should rest

your tired feet,

my tiny *ballerina star.*

Fold your leotard and tutu.

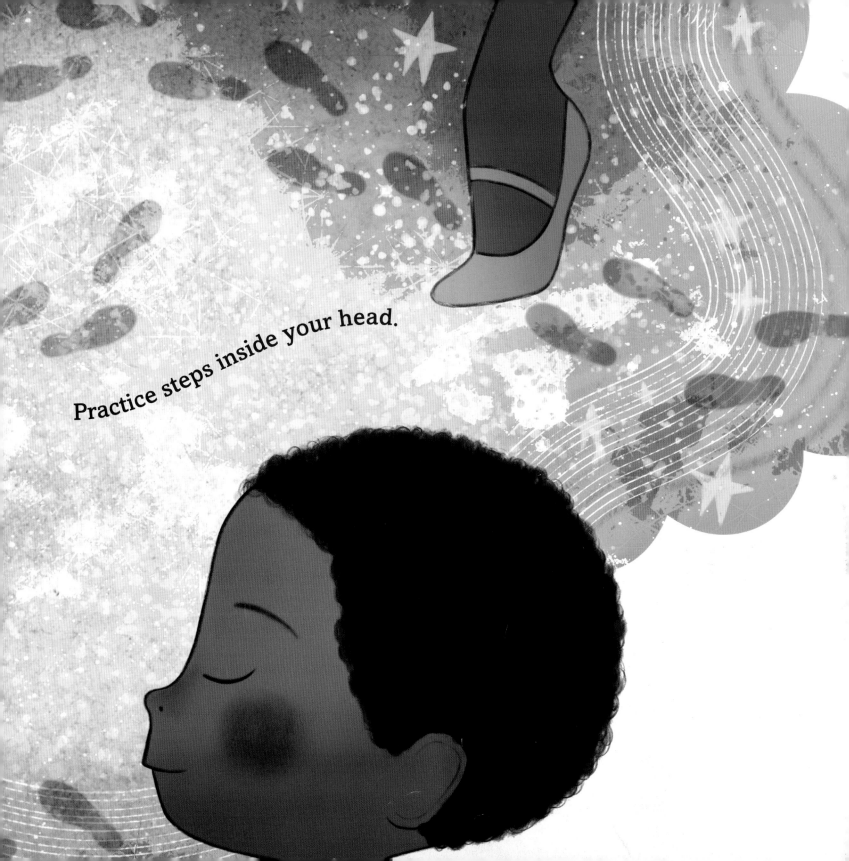

Practice steps inside your head.

Tomorrow you'll be on the stage.

But now let's tuck you into bed.

Imagine stretching, bending, leaping,

pirouetting on moonbeams.

Goodnight, now, my darling dancer.

Twirl your way into your dreams.